W9-BOH-149

For Aaron, Oshie and Luke

(and all the Alices of the world)

Roaring, Boring Alice: A Story of the Aurora Borealis

Story by: P.K. Merski
Illustrated by: Mark Weber
Designed by: Tungsten Creative Group

ISBN: 0-9747217-0-0
Library of Congress: 2004090342
Printed in Hong Kong
Price: $16.95/USA
Keywords: Aurora Borealis; Choice; Rhyming Story; Behavior; Fantasy; Picture Book

Check out www.roaringboringalice.com

Roaring, Boring Alice

A Story of the Aurora Borealis

Oh, that

roaring, boring
Alice...

What a pest she could **be**.
She had nothin' to do,
No place to go,

No friends,
hardly any...

except **me**.

There was just something about her that really made you sore.
To Alice everything was awful, everyone a bore.

"This soup's too hot; my peas are cold," she informed mother diligently.
That's the night she got it...I say fin-al-ly.

"To your room!"

Mother replied with an evil eye on her;
"And stay there till I call you!"
(which I hoped would be a year.)

And so Alice stormed
up the stairs with a roar!
The windows shook when she
slammed the door!

She cleared her bed;
Stuffed animals flew!
She was fuming mad again.
So what else is new?

I sneaked up behind her.
Crawled under the door...
Ever so slowly.

(Like a snail on the floor.)

Now, from under
the bed I had a good view
of Alice—Oh my goodness—her face was **blue!**

And
as Alice
prepared
her next
piercing shout,
She opened
her mouth...

but
nothing
came
out.

Then, streamers of light suddenly
bloomed from her face,
Colors began flowing
all over the place.

A strange little person with a very stern voice
appeared out of nowhere to give Alice a choice:

"I have come from Agartha,
the subterranean world,
and across our night sky
your voice has been hurled.

Every sound from your mouth
has been changed into lights
to color our sky on clear, star-lit nights.

If you want your voice back
Alice, my dear,
Be nice!
And the colors will all disappear!"

By now, Alice saw me—there—under the bed,
She tried to cry out, but her voice had turned red.
Streams of colors—
Yellow! Green! Orange! And blue!
All flowed from her lips,
such a spectacular hue.

Colors the shape of
butterfly
wings
bounced off the walls
and colored her things.

Outside past
the window
flashed red
and green.
As the
heavens
displayed
a dazzling
scene.

Then
colorful
fingers
pointed
my gaze,
to the top
of the sky
where her
voice was
ablaze!

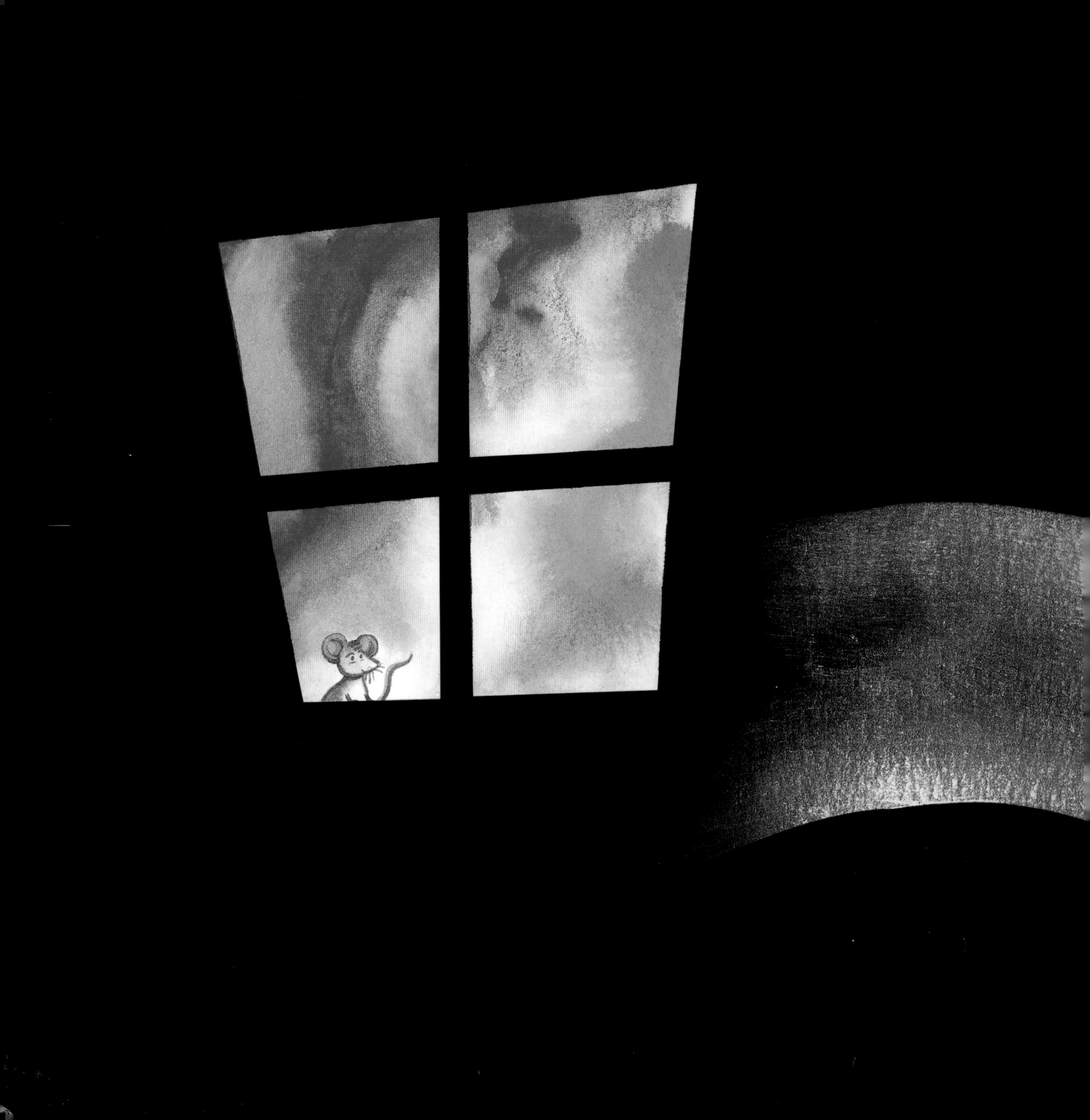

And that strange little
person simply floated away,
on a wave of blue light
he moved with a sway.

Alice sat crossed legged,
amid toys on the floor,
all silently enjoying her
technicolor roar.

When a single long,
seemingly endless tear dripped
Off her chin, down her neck
where her voice had been stripped.

That's when it happened...

(that instant, that night).

Alice settled down
after her colorful fright.
In her silence, the colors
were now barely seen
And the room was a
peaceful, motionless green.

She picked up
her Cha-Cha,
cleared her throat
for the test—

"I'm sorry,"
she peeped,
"I wasn't acting
my best!"

Then she tidied her room, a bright smile on her face
For her voice and the colors were now back in place.
She returned to the table feeling quite fresh and new
And ever so quietly she whispered.

"Thank you."

Now, every once in awhile,
(I'd say twice a year)
Alice starts roaring
and the Agartheans hear.
It's on those clear nights
especially due north
That the pitch of her voice
sets these colors forth.
The sky suddenly opens
its red, blue-green palace
And millions of eyes
enjoy the

Aurora Borealis!

About the Aurora Borealis

The aurora borealis is produced in the ionosphere when atomic particles strike and excite atoms. The colors depend on the type of atoms and molecules struck by the energetic particles, raining down along the earth's magnetic field. The brightest and most common color is yellowish-green, which appears about sixty miles up in the sky. The rare, all-red auroras appear about 200 miles high. Some of the more common shapes are described as curtains, veils, tapestries, fingers, snakes, coronas, fox tails or streamers. Although the aurora borealis appears nightly, it is often too dim to see. There are studies showing that the aurora borealis has a voice of its own! Swishing and crackling, spark-like noises have been captured and recorded by students and scientists. Auroras occur along ring-shaped areas of the north and south poles. Fairbanks, Alaska is under this region in North America, so it is a good place to watch the northern lights. In the Southern Hemisphere, these colorful lights are called the Aurora Australis and are visible in areas around the South Pole.

Mini Glossary of Terms

Agartha: The imaginary home of an advanced civilization, believed to be located under the North Pole.

Agartheans: People who live in Agartha.

Cha cha: Alice's favorite stuffed animal, her monkey

Ionosphere: The outermost layer of the earth's atmosphere, it contains layers of different particles, mainly electrons.

Northern Lights: Another name for aurora borealis

Subterranean: Beneath the earth's surface

For more information on the aurora borealis go to www.roaringboringalice.com.